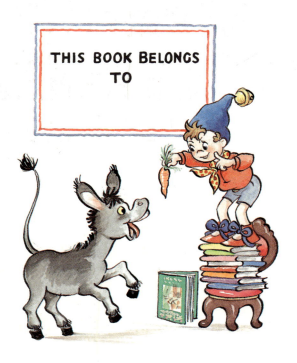

THIS BOOK BELONGS TO

Published by BBC Books,
an imprint of BBC Worldwide Publishing.
BBC Worldwide Ltd., Woodlands, 80 Wood Lane, London W12 0TT

First published 1960 by Sampson Lowe

This edition 1992
Reprinted 1994, 1995
© Darrell Waters Limited 1960 as to all text and illustrations

Enid Blyton's signature mark and the word 'NODDY'
are Registered Trade Marks of Darrell Waters Limited

ISBN 0 563 36839 X

Printed in Great Britain by BPC Paulton Books Limited.

CHEER UP LITTLE NODDY!

BY *Enid Blyton*

CONTENTS

1. Two Bad Little Bears
2. Everyone is Kind to Noddy
3. Noddy is Very, Very Busy
4. The Saucepan Man
5. Noddy and the Donkey
6. Stop it, Bumpy-Dog!
7. Hurray! Hurray!

BBC BOOKS

NODDY RODE ON THE DONKEY'S BACK AND WAVED
PROUDLY TO EVERYONE HE MET

1. TWO BAD LITTLE BEARS

NODDY was washing his little car one morning, singing very loudly because he felt so happy. He splashed water about, and the car jiggled and hooted because it felt happy too.

Noddy sang and sang, and rubbed and polished, his head nodding all the time. It was nice to hear him.

> "The sun is shining
> And so is my car,
> It's a beautiful morning,
> How happy we are!
> Parp-parp-parp!

CHEER UP LITTLE NODDY!

Soon we'll be speeding
Away down the street,
Hooting and waving
To friends that we meet,
Parp-parp-parp!

And now I have finished,
So in I will jump,
And drive away quickly,
A-bumpety-bump,
Parp-parp-parp!"

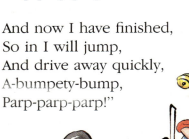

The little car joined in at the "parp-parps", and jiggled happily. Just as Noddy was giving it the very last rub, someone called to him.

"Hallo, Noddy! Can we help you?"

Noddy looked round and saw little Tubby Bear leaning on the wall, with another little bear beside him.

"Well, I've just finished," said Noddy. "Who's that bear with you?"

"My cousin, Tommy Bear," said Tubby. "He's

TWO BAD LITTLE BEARS

come to spend the day with me. Do you think he could just sit in your car for a minute? He loves cars."

"I can drive," said Tommy Bear, proudly.

"Well, you needn't think I'll let you drive *my* car," said Noddy. "You can just *sit* in it, and nothing else. Tubby, sit with him, and don't let him do anything silly. I'm going to wash my hands, and take off my overalls—then I'm going out to look for passengers."

Noddy went into his little house, whistling. Tubby Bear and Tommy Bear jumped over the wall in delight, and ran to where the little car stood outside Noddy's garage in the sunshine. Tommy Bear climbed into the driver's seat, and pressed the hooter. "PARP-PARP-PARP-PARP-PARP!"

CHEER UP LITTLE NODDY!

"Stop that noise!" yelled Noddy, putting his head out of the window. "Get out, Tommy Bear. Stop hooting. GET OUT, I SAY!"

But Tommy was *not* going to get out. He was enjoying himself. How lovely to sit in such a dear little car, and hoot as if it belonged to him!

Then a very naughty thought came into Tommy's head. If only he could drive the car just a *little* way! Just down the road and back. He whispered into Tubby's ear, and Tubby nodded at once. "I'll have a turn too," he said.

So, to the little car's enormous surprise, Tommy Bear drove it out into the road! The car was very cross. It didn't like being driven by anyone but Noddy. It began to hoot loudly, trying to tell Noddy what was happening, and Noddy put his head out of the window, ready to shout at the two little bears again.

He could not believe his eyes when he saw his little car going

TOMMY BEAR DROVE THE LITTLE CAR OUT
INTO THE ROAD!

CHEER UP LITTLE NODDY!

down the road—slowly at first, then faster, and then very fast indeed!

"Stop, little car, stop! Come back!" shouted Noddy, running out of his front gate. He was just in time to see the car turn a corner at top speed, hooting furiously. Noddy ran out into the road, feeling quite shocked. "Tommy Bear will have an accident! I know he will!" said poor Noddy, nodding his head up and down very fast indeed.

The two little bears were enjoying themselves. They raced into the High Street, where everyone was busy shopping. The little car was still hooting angrily. Mr Plod the policeman was standing in the middle of the road, directing the traffic. He was most astonished to see Noddy's car coming straight for him at top speed.

TWO BAD LITTLE BEARS

"What do you think you are doing, Noddy?" he yelled, and jumped aside just in time, falling over with a bump! He stared after the little car in surprise. "It *wasn't* Noddy driving!" he said. "Who was it then? Wait till I get hold of him! Somebody is going to be in an awful lot of trouble!"

Poor Noddy was still standing in the road, wondering what to do. "No good going after my car," he said to himself. "I don't even know where it is. How DARE that nasty little Tommy Bear drive it away? And to think Tubby Bear let him! I'll teach them! I'll pull their noses! I'll tread on their toes! I'll—well, no, I'd better not. I'll go and tell Mr Plod, he'll know what to do!"

CHEER UP LITTLE NODDY!

So Noddy set off to find Mr Plod—but on the way he met Big-Ears, riding his bicycle very fast, and ringing his bell loudly. "Ting-a-ling-a-ting-a-ling-a-ling-a-ting!"

"Big-Ears! BIG-EARS! Stop! I've got something to tell you!" shouted Noddy. Big-Ears put on his brakes and stopped so suddenly that he nearly flew over the handle-bars.

"Noddy! I was looking for you!" he cried. "Noddy, there's been an accident. Oh, Noddy, your poor little car! Those two bad bears ran it into a tree near my Toadstool House and..."

"Big-Ears—where is it? Is it badly hurt?" cried Noddy, and big tears ran down his cheeks. "Oh, I was afraid this would happen! What about the little bears?"

"Not even scratched or bruised!" said Big-Ears. "They jumped out and ran away—but wait till I see them again... I'll—I'll—well, I really don't know *what* I'll do!"

2. EVERYONE IS KIND TO NODDY

BIG-EARS and Noddy went off to kind Mr Sparks, who owned the garage in Toy Town. He was very upset to hear about Noddy's car. "I'll bring the breakdown van up to Big-Ears' house and collect it," he said. "Now don't you worry—I'll soon have it mended for you!"

Oh dear, oh dear—when Noddy saw his poor little car he was very sad indeed. The front was smashed in, and the lamps were broken, and one wheel was almost off. Noddy cried when he saw it, but Mr Sparks comforted him, and so did Big-Ears.

CHEER UP LITTLE NODDY!

"It can be mended!" said Mr Sparks. "I'll make it as good as new."

"It can't even say 'Parp-parp' to me," wept Noddy.

"Parp-parp," said the car suddenly, in a small hoarse voice, and Noddy went to stroke it and pat it, just as if it were a dog.

"Don't worry!" he said to his little car. "I'll see that you are mended, even if it costs me all the money I earn in a year. I'll drive you again, little car, so don't be sad. You'll be back home in your little garage again soon!"

"Parp-parp!" said the little car once more, sounding happier. Soon kind Mr Sparks had lifted it on

to his breakdown van, and driven off through Toadstool Wood. Noddy stayed behind with Big-Ears, who made some hot cocoa, and put some

EVERYONE IS KIND TO NODDY

big slices of fruit cake on his little table. Whiskers the cat came and sat on Noddy's knee, purring loudly, and rubbing his big soft head against him.

"He's telling me to eat some fruit cake and feel better," said Noddy to Big-Ears. "So I think I will. Big-Ears, what shall I do to earn money now that my car is broken?"

"Well now, let's think," said Big-Ears, helping himself to a piece of cake. "You could borrow a barrow, and do people's shopping for them, bringing everything back in the barrow."

"Oh *yes* — and I could charge sixpence a time," said Noddy, drinking his cocoa.

"And you could go to the market and buy flowers and fruit cheaply, and sell them to anyone in Toy Town who wants them," said Big-Ears.

CHEER UP LITTLE NODDY!

"You could charge an extra penny on everything you sell, to pay for your trouble."

"Dear me—you do have some good ideas, Big-Ears," said Noddy, pleased. "I'll barrow a borrow tomorrow—I mean, I'll morrow a borrow tomarrow—no, no—I'll borrow a marrow tomorrow—oh, Big-Ears, aren't I silly? I can't say it right!"

Big-Ears laughed, and Noddy began to laugh too. "*That's* better!" said Big-Ears. "Laughing is better than crying any day. Well—borrow a marrow, or morrow a barrow—whichever you like—so long as you can wheel goods in it and earn money! Have another slice of cake."

Noddy felt much better when he left Big-Ears and Whiskers, and went off back to Toy Town again. Everyone he met came up to tell him how sorry they were about his car, and they all promised to give him errands to do if he could borrow a barrow.

BIG-EARS LAUGHED, AND NODDY BEGAN
TO LAUGH TOO

CHEER UP LITTLE NODDY!

"Mr Tubby Bear will lend you his," said Miss Fluffy Cat. "He and Mrs Tubby Bear are so very sorry about your car, Noddy. Tubby Bear has been sent to bed already, and it serves him right—and Tommy Bear has disappeared. He's afraid to go back to the Tubby Bears', and he hasn't gone home, either. Nobody knows where he is, the little nuisance."

"Just let me catch him!" said Noddy, fiercely. "I'll pull his hair, I'll tread on his toes, I'll . . ."

"That won't bring your car back, Noddy," said Miss Fluffy Cat. "I expect he's very sorry now and is afraid to show his furry face."

Noddy went to Mr Tubby to ask if he would lend him his barrow. "Of course!" said Mr Tubby,

EVERYONE IS KIND TO NODDY

putting his big arm round Noddy. "We'll help you all we can, Noddy. Tubby Bear has been sent to bed as a punishment, and he wants to give you the money out of his money box to help pay the bill for mending your car. But I'm afraid it will be a very *big* bill, Noddy. Mrs Tubby Bear says she'll do all your washing for you and your mending too, to show how sorry *she* is."

It wasn't only the Tubby Bears who were kind. Little Tessie Bear came hurrying to see Noddy when she heard the news. She hugged him tightly, and the Bumpy-Dog, who had come with her, licked Noddy so much that he had to get a towel to wipe his face.

"Bumpy, don't!" said Noddy. "I know you lick me because you like me, but your tongue's so *wet!*

CHEER UP LITTLE NODDY!

I shall have to keep a towel in my pocket instead of a hanky if you go on like this! Oooh—DON'T jump up at me like that! You'll knock me over!"

"BUMPY! Go outside," said Tessie Bear, and Bumpy put down his tail and trotted out, looking very upset. "He wants to say he's sorry too," said Tessie. "But he's so *very* excitable. Dear Noddy—I'll help you all I can. I'll take one handle of Mr Tubby's barrow, and help you to wheel it."

"Oh no, Tessie—I couldn't let you do that," said Noddy. "I'm very strong. Feel my arms—they're as hard as anything!"

"Yes, they seem quite strong," said Tessie, feeling Noddy's little wooden arms. "Noddy, I've brought you some toffee. I made it myself for you."

EVERYONE IS KIND TO NODDY

People really were very kind to Noddy. Miss Fluffy Cat sent him a meat pie she had baked, and Sally Skittle sent her children along with some lovely jam tarts. It was a pity

that the Bumpy-Dog was at the gate when the Skittle family came because he thought the tarts were for him. He had eaten seven by the time Noddy came out!

Then the Wobbly Man wobbled along with a box of chocolates. The Bumpy-Dog leapt at him in delight, and the Wobbly Man wobbled to and fro so much that he dropped all the chocolates on the

CHEER UP LITTLE NODDY!

ground. The Bumpy-Dog was very pleased!

But Noddy wasn't. He chased Bumpy away with a stick, and Bumpy fled in horror. A stick! Oh no, he wasn't going to stay if Noddy had a stick! He went back to Tessie Bear's and put himself to bed in his kennel, wishing he had had time to lick up a few more of those chocolates.

3. NODDY IS VERY, VERY BUSY

NEXT day Noddy was very, very busy. He took Mr Tubby's barrow and went to ask for jobs. He sang a little song as he went.

"Parcels fetched
And shopping done,
Letters posted,
Errands run!

Windows cleaned
And doorsteps too,
Goods delivered,
All day through!

If you're wanting
Cakes for tea,
Or eggs for supper,
Shout for ME!"

CHEER UP LITTLE NODDY!

Well, so many people wanted to help Noddy that he soon had more jobs than he could do! Tessie Bear met him in the town, wheeling Mr Tubby Bear's big barrow. It was full of shopping. Noddy puffed and panted as he pushed the barrow along.

"Noddy! Come and have an ice-cream," said Tessie. "You look hot."

"Well, I *am* hot!" said Noddy. "But I'm earning a lot of money, Tessie. I think I'll soon be able to pay for my car being mended. I don't think I'll stop for an ice-cream, thank you. I promised Mrs Skittle I'd take all her shopping home in time for the Skittle children's dinner."

Off he went, wheeling the heavy barrow. Tessie Bear stared after him. "Oh dear—he'll tire himself out," she thought. "He's so little, and the barrow is so BIG!"

"NODDY! COME AND HAVE AN ICE-CREAM,"
SAID TESSIE

CHEER UP LITTLE NODDY!

Noddy really did work hard that first day. The second day was worse, because Mr Noah sent Katie Kangaroo to him, to ask if he would please fetch all the food for the Noah's Ark animals that day.

"Good gracious!" said Noddy. "It won't all go into my barrow, Katie Kangaroo, even if I pile it up high."

"Well, you could fill the barrow a second time, couldn't you?" said Katie. "I'll come along with you and carry some things in my pouch."

But even with Katie's help, there were still three barrow-loads of food to take to the Ark. Noddy began to feel as if his arms would fall off. Mrs Noah was sorry for him. "Can't you get a little hand-

cart?" she said. "That would be easier for you than pushing a heavy barrow."

NODDY IS VERY, VERY BUSY

So Noddy borrowed a little hand-cart from Tessie's Uncle Bear the next day, and found it a bit easier, because he could pull it along behind him instead of having to push it like a barrow.

But still he panted and puffed! Noddy pulled the little four-wheeled cart about all day long, fetching shopping, posting parcels, and collecting washing for such a lot of people.

Big-Ears gave him a job too. "Will you collect a box for me at the railway station?" he said. "It will have a new tea-set in it, so be careful, Noddy. I'll pay you a whole shilling if you bring it up to my house without breaking anything."

So Noddy collected the big box from the porter at the railway station just after the train had gone. Goodness—it was heavy! It took both Noddy *and* the porter to carry it to the little hand-cart.

"My word—I hope you haven't very far to take this heavy box," said the porter.

"Well, I *have!*" said Noddy. "It's for Big-Ears, my friend, and he lives right in the middle of Toadstool Wood. I shall certainly need to sit down by

CHEER UP LITTLE NODDY!

the time I get there! I'll sit in his comfy armchair for an hour, I should think!"

Poor little Noddy! He panted and puffed up the path through the wood to Big-Ears' house, and all the little rabbits came out to watch him. Two rabbits tried to help him with the cart, but he hadn't even enough breath to say thank you!

At last Noddy reached Big-Ears' front door and knocked. Then he sat down on the path, panting.

Big-Ears opened the door. "Oh, you good little Noddy!" he said, pleased. "You've brought my new tea-set safely. Help me in with it."

"I can't," said Noddy, in a very small voice. "I can't get up. My legs won't let me. They're so tired."

"Noddy! You poor little fellow!" cried Big-Ears, and ran to help him. "Come along — lean

NODDY IS VERY, VERY BUSY

on me. I've a fine tea waiting for you."

"I don't want any," said Noddy. "I'm too tired to eat. My teeth won't bite, and my throat won't swallow."

"Dear me—how silly we've all been, giving you so many jobs to do, thinking we were helping you!" said Big-Ears, settling Noddy into his best armchair. "There now — lie back, and shut your eyes. I'll make the tea and butter the scones."

"I can't eat any scones," said Noddy, still speaking in a very small voice, and at once he fell asleep. Big-Ears stood and looked at him.

"Poor little Noddy! Working so hard! And after all, it wasn't *his* fault that his car had to be mended. Tubby Bear and Tommy Bear ought to be doing all this work, not Noddy. But those lazy little bears would probably sit down and rest half the time!" Big-Ears frowned, and then looked out of the window at the four-wheeled hand-cart with the big box inside.

CHEER UP LITTLE NODDY!

"Noddy can't pull that about all day long. It's too heavy. I wonder if I could get a horse to pull it for him. A nice *little* horse. No—I don't know anyone with a horse to lend. What a pity!" Big-Ears let Noddy sleep. He carried the box from the hand-cart into his house and began to unpack the tea-set. Not one single thing was broken. Noddy still slept on and on, cuddled down in the armchair.

Then away in the distance Big-Ears heard a loud voice calling. Who ever was this coming along? He listened hard, and heard a song he knew very well.

"I'm the Saucepan Man, the Saucepan Man,
I can sell you a kettle or a pan,
Or a nice little watering can,
Because I am the Saucepan Man.
Saucepans for SALE!
Saucepans for SALE!"

4. THE SAUCEPAN MAN

"THAT'S the Saucepan Man," said Big-Ears, pleased. "He must have known I wanted a new saucepan and a kettle as well. And his dear little donkey, Ee-Aw, is with him too. Good!"

He went to the door and shouted. "Hey, Saucepan Man. Come and have some tea!"

The Saucepan Man came up, beaming all over his jolly face. He was hung about with saucepans and kettles and pans, which made a tremendous jingling, clattering noise. The noise was quite deafening and it had made the Saucepan Man very hard of hearing.

Trotting behind him was his little donkey, Ee-Aw, hung about with saucepans and kettles, too. What a noise they made as they came up the path — clitter, clatter, jingle, jangle, clippity-clop.

CHEER UP LITTLE NODDY!

"Hallo, Mr Saucepan," said Big-Ears. "Come in. Tea's just ready. I've Noddy here too, but he's asleep."

Soon Big-Ears and Mr Saucepan were eating hot scones, and Mr Saucepan was telling Big-Ears all about his adventures. "I wish Noddy would wake up and have some tea too," said Big-Ears. "Oh look at Ee-Aw peeping in at the window. May I give him a hot scone?"

Mr Saucepan was so deaf that when Big-Ears spoke to him he had to shout at the top of his voice—but not even the shouting awoke Noddy. He slept on and on and on.

"Big-Ears, I've come to ask you something," said Mr Saucepan, eating his fifth scone. "I want your help. I'm going to visit my Old Aunt Katie Kettle— have I ever told you about her? She lives over the sea."

THE SAUCEPAN MAN

"Good gracious! Are you going off in a boat then?" said Big-Ears. "Whatever will Ee-Aw the donkey say to that?"

"Well, he just won't *come*," said Mr Saucepan. "I've talked and talked to him about it, but he shakes his head every time and stamps his hoof. You just see!" He turned to where Ee-Aw was still staring in at the window and called to him. "Ee-Aw—you *will* come in a boat with me across the sea, won't you?"

Ee-Aw at once shook his head firmly from side to side, and stamped his hoof. "There you are," said Mr Saucepan. "He just *won't* come. He must be frightened of crabs or something. Anyway, I've come to ask you if you'll please look after him for me while I am gone."

"Look after your *donkey!*" said Big-Ears. "Of course not. Don't be silly. I've nowhere to keep a *donkey*. You can't go about asking people to look after donkeys, you know."

"Well, I kept Whiskers, your cat, for you, and looked after him once, when *you* went away," said Mr Saucepan.

35

CHEER UP LITTLE NODDY!

"That's different," said Big-Ears. "A donkey is *much* bigger than a cat, Mr Saucepan. Perhaps you haven't noticed that?"

"Oh well—I'll go and ask someone else to have Ee-Aw," said Mr Saucepan, in a huff, and got up with a great clatter and jingle. "He's quite useful. He'll give people rides, or carry sacks of potatoes and things like that. Goodbye, Big-Ears. I won't catch any fish for you when I'm at sea. You'd probably say they were too big for you to cook for your dinner. Goodbye!"

Just as Mr Saucepan was walking out of the door, looking very cross, a Good Idea came to Big-Ears and he yelled loudly after the Saucepan Man.

"MR SAUCEPAN! MR SAUCEPAN! I'VE GOT A WONDERFUL IDEA!"
YELLED BIG-EARS

CHEER UP LITTLE NODDY!

"Mr Saucepan! MR SAUCEPAN! I've got a wonderful idea! Come back! I'll look after your donkey for you—or at least my friend Noddy here will look after him—and use him too! MR SAUCEPAN, stop being cross and COME BACK!"

Mr Saucepan came back, looking surprised. "Did I hear you shouting at me?" he said. "What do you want?"

Big-Ears told him all over again, and Mr Saucepan looked pleased. "All right. I'll leave Ee-Aw with you," he said. "He'll be quite good. He likes you. I really must go, Big-Ears, or I shall miss my train."

"Train? But I thought you were going over the sea!" said Big-Ears, astonished.

"Dear me, yes—so I am," said Mr Saucepan. "Good thing you reminded me. I've a boat to catch, of course, not a train. Goodbye, Big-Ears. Be kind to Ee-Aw. I'll soon be back."

5. NODDY AND THE DONKEY

BIG-EARS went out to see the Saucepan Man off. While he was at the front gate, waving goodbye, Noddy woke up. He was MOST surprised to see a donkey's face looking in at the window.

"What a nice little donkey!" he said. "Looking in at the window too! I must still be asleep and dreaming. Hallo, little donkey!"

"Ee-aw, ee-aw," said the donkey, waving his long, furry ears about. Big-Ears came back just then, and Noddy called out to him.

"Oh—Big-Ears, *you're* in my dream, too, as well as the donkey. Isn't he sweet! I wish he were mine!"

"You *aren't* dreaming," said Big-Ears. "That's a *real* donkey, Noddy. It belongs to old Mr Saucepan. And do you know what? You can borrow him

CHEER UP LITTLE NODDY!

to carry all your shopping and parcels!"

"*Borrow* him! Borrow a *donkey!*" said Noddy, in great astonishment. "This must be a dream! Nobody's ever offered to lend me a donkey before. I wish I *were* awake! It would be such a help to have a donkey to carry all my packages and parcels. My poor arms are so very tired."

"You poor little fellow!" said Big-Ears. "What have we all been thinking of, letting you work so hard! It's true about the donkey, Noddy. Mr Saucepan has gone to visit his Aunt Katie Kettle over the sea, and he's left his donkey with me. You can use him to carry all your things."

"Oh, I'm so happy!" said Noddy, running to Big-Ears. "To think I won't have to push a barrow or pull a cart any more! Thank you, Big-Ears, thank you! Oh, I must go and talk to the donkey. What's his name? Can I bring him indoors?"

"No, certainly not," said Big-Ears. "There wouldn't be much left of my little house if Ee-Aw gallivanted round it!"

"Oh, does he gallivant?" said Noddy. "What's

NODDY AND THE DONKEY

gallivanting? Can *I* gallivant? I'll gallivant out to speak to Ee-Aw! Watch me gallivant, Big-Ears! Oh, I'm so happy again!"

Ee-Aw was delighted to see little Noddy, and butted him gently with his nose. Noddy flung his arms round the donkey's neck and hugged him.

"Ee-aw!" said the donkey, in delight, and suddenly did a little dance, clip-clopping all over the place. Big-Ears laughed. Well, well—now everything would be fine! Noddy would have someone to carry his things, and pull his little cart—and Ee-Aw would be happy while the Saucepan Man was away.

"Big-Ears, I could eat some tea now," said Noddy. "I suddenly don't feel tired any more. And

CHEER UP LITTLE NODDY!

after tea Ee-Aw and I are going to gallivant down to Toy Town, and fetch some things for Mr Noah. Ee-Aw says he knows how to gallivant. He nodded his head when I asked him. Big-Ears, isn't he a DEAR little donkey?"

Well, Noddy had a wonderful time now that he had a donkey to help him. He rode down to Toy Town, with Ee-Aw dragging the little hand-cart along behind him, and how everyone stared to see Noddy riding on a donkey!

Noddy sang a merry song as they trotted down the street.

"Oh, I've a little donkey
That gallivants along,
I know he's rather little,
But he's very, VERY strong!
He can trot and canter,
He can say 'ee-aw!'
He's just the nicest donkey
I ever, ever saw!
EE-AW! EE-AW!

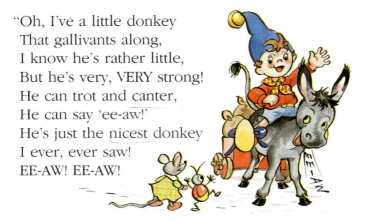

NODDY AND THE DONKEY

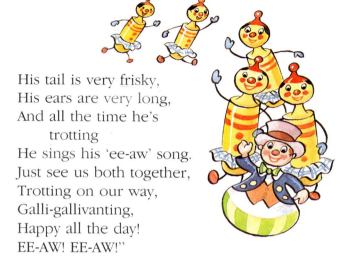

His tail is very frisky,
His ears are very long,
And all the time he's
   trotting
He sings his 'ee-aw' song.
Just see us both together,
Trotting on our way,
Galli-gallivanting,
Happy all the day!
EE-AW! EE-AW!"

Every time Noddy came to the ee-aw part, the little donkey joined in. The Skittle children ran after him, delighted, and the Wobbly Man wobbled as fast as he could to keep up with him. As for Mr Plod, he couldn't believe his eyes when he suddenly saw Noddy trotting by at top speed on a *donkey*.

"Hey—what do you think you're doing on that donkey?" shouted Mr Plod.

"I'm gallivanting!" shouted Noddy. "We're *both* gallivanting! You come and gallivant too, Mr Plod!"

CHEER UP LITTLE NODDY!

Everyone gathered round to pat the little donkey, and promised Noddy to give him plenty of goods to deliver the next day.

"I can put your parcels and sacks in this little cart that Ee-Aw is dragging behind him," said Noddy. "Then I'll ride on his back, and it won't take us any time to take the goods here and there. Isn't he lovely?"

Everyone agreed that Ee-Aw *was* a lovely donkey indeed. Tessie Bear rushed into the greengrocer's shop and bought him a carrot. Ee-Aw was very pleased. He ate the carrot, and then tried to eat the flowers round Tessie's hat.

"No, Ee-Aw, no!" said Noddy. "Look out, Tessie, he might eat your hat as well as the flowers! We'd better go, I think. He's getting a bit frisky—what Big-Ears would call *gallivanty*. Come on, Ee-Aw, gallivant away. That's right—clip-clop-clippetty-clop—ooh, mind that monkey, you nearly trod on his tail!"

"COME ON, EE-AW, GALLIVANT AWAY," CRIED NODDY.
"OH MIND THAT MONKEY!"

CHEER UP LITTLE NODDY!

Noddy came to his little House-For-One and slid down off Ee-Aw's furry back. Ee-Aw liked the look of the house very much, and trotted straight up the path to the door.

"Ee-Aw, I really think you'd better go into the garage," said Noddy. "My dear little car has had an accident, so the garage is empty. I don't think you'd behave very well inside a house."

But Ee-Aw had other ideas. He wanted to see Noddy's house, and as soon as Noddy opened the door, he trotted in, braying in delight.

"Ee-aw, ee-aw, nicest house I ever saw!" he seemed to say, and sat down on one of Noddy's chairs. But he was much too heavy, and the chair creaked and broke. Ee-Aw was dreadfully upset, and ran straight out of the house braying mournfully.

NODDY AND THE DONKEY

Noddy ran after him, shouting, "It's all right, Ee-Aw, I forgive you! PLEASE don't run away! Ee-Aw, I'll give you carrots for your supper. EE-AW, COME BACK."

Then the little donkey trotted back, hanging his head in shame. He went straight into the garage this time, and lay down on the floor.

"I'll bring you some straw to lie on, for a nice bed," said Noddy. "And I'll leave the door open so that you won't be in the dark. But don't gallivant away, will you? Oh, I *do* like that word. Gallivant, gallivant, gallivant away, I'd like to go a-gallivanting, every single day! That's a new song I've made up for *you*, Ee-Aw."

CHEER UP LITTLE NODDY!

Soon Noddy had brought some straw for Ee-Aw, and pulled some new carrots from his garden. Mrs Tubby Bear was most astonished to see a donkey in the garage. She was still feeling very sorry about Tubby and Tommy taking Noddy's car, and she had brought Noddy a lovely iced cake.

"Ee-aw!" said the donkey, joyfully, thinking it was for him. Noddy just saved the cake in time!

"No—this is for *me!*" he said. "The *carrots* are for you! Oh, Ee-Aw—what fun we'll have tomorrow when we go round delivering our goods and parcels together!"

6. STOP IT, BUMPY-DOG!

NODDY awoke very early the next morning, hearing a most peculiar noise nearby. He sat up in bed and listened. "Cloppetty-clippetty-cloppetty-clip, cloppetty . . ."

"Goodness—it's Ee-Aw doing a little gallivant round my garage!" said Noddy. "He'll wake everyone up!"

So he went out to the garage and opened the door. Ee-Aw was so pleased to see Noddy that he ran straight at him, and knocked him over.

"You're as bad as the Bumpy-Dog!" said Noddy. "Ee-Aw, stop racing round the garage. You're making a terrible noise, and it's not even six o'clock yet."

"Ee-aw, ee-aw!" said the donkey, rubbing his nose lovingly against Noddy's shoulder. Then he snuffled gently into Noddy's ear. Noddy

CHEER UP LITTLE NODDY!

couldn't help liking him—he really was a *dear* little donkey!

"Come into my house—but be very quiet, because I want to go to sleep again," said Noddy. "We've a hard day's work to do, you know." He led Ee-Aw into his house, and the donkey at once lay down on the floor, afraid of trying to sit on a chair again. Noddy climbed into bed.

Ee-Aw put his head on the pillow to be as near Noddy as he could, and he went to sleep too. When the milkman came, and looked in at the window, he was *most* astonished. Whatever next!

Noddy and the donkey had a very busy time that day! Everyone came hurrying up with goods to be taken here and there, lists of shopping for Noddy to do, and orders for him to go to the market and buy fruit and vegetables for them.

STOP IT, BUMPY-DOG!

Noddy felt very important indeed. He set off with Ee-Aw, the little hand-cart trundling along behind them. Soon it was full of parcels and sacks. Noddy rode on the donkey's back, and waved proudly to everyone he met.

Then the Bumpy-Dog came running by and suddenly saw Noddy high up on the donkey's back. He simply couldn't believe it! He hadn't heard anything about Ee-Aw and was most excited to see Noddy riding him.

He raced up, barking wildly. "Wuff-WUFF-WUFFY-WUFF!" Ee-Aw got a terrible fright. He began to gallop at top speed, with the Bumpy-Dog chasing after him.

CHEER UP LITTLE NODDY!

The little cart bumped along, jolting here and there, and one by one all the parcels and sacks shot out into the road. Noddy was very angry indeed. He pulled at the donkey's ears, and yelled at Bumpy-Dog.

"Stop it, Bumpy-Dog! Have you gone mad? Bumpy, GO AWAY! Stop Ee-Aw! My goodness, they're both as bad as each other! Oh, my parcels and sacks! Bumpy, GO AWAY! Oh dear, now here's Mr Plod. Ee-Aw, stop! STOP!"

But Ee-Aw didn't stop, and Mr Plod suddenly found himself sitting down hard in the road, while a mad donkey, a little mad nodding man, a mad dog and a mad hand-cart raced by him at sixty miles an hour. Mr Plod was very, very angry. He stared after the cloud of dust in the distance.

"Was that NODDY on that donkey again?

STOP IT, BUMPY-DOG!

What in the world does he think he's doing? I'll put him in prison! As for that Bumpy-Dog, he ought to live in a kennel without any door! Where's my helmet?"

"Please, Mr Plod, you're sitting on it," said Katie Kitten, with a giggle. "Mr Plod, shall I pick up all the things that have fallen out of Noddy's cart?"

Well, Katie Kitten, Miss Fluffy Cat and Sally Skittle all helped to pick up the things that had fallen out of Noddy's cart. Then they waited for Noddy and Ee-Aw to come back.

"There they are," said Katie. "Goodness, doesn't Noddy look cross!"

He certainly did. He was cross with Ee-Aw and cross with Bumpy and cross with everybody.

"What's the good of me trying to help everyone?" he shouted. "My donkey ran away, Bumpy-Dog went mad, and my little cart and all

CHEER UP LITTLE NODDY!

my parcels are gone! Mr Plod, arrest the Bumpy-Dog and put him in prison!"

Mr Plod had never seen Noddy so angry before. "Now, now!" he said. "Calm yourself, Noddy. I can see it wasn't your fault that I was knocked down. All your parcels are safe. But where is your cart?"

"Goodness knows!" said Noddy. "But I'm not going to use it again while I have Ee-Aw! Galloping away like that with a cart full of things! He'll have to carry them on his back in future and I shall walk beside him, holding his bridle firmly. What with a gallivanting donkey, and a

gallivanting dog, I'm — I'm — well, I feel as if *I* want to gallivant too, and knock everyone down!"

Tessie Bear came up then, and laughed. She slipped her little paw into Noddy's hand. "Don't worry, Noddy! And don't be cross any more.

STOP IT, BUMPY-DOG!

We'll all help to put the things on Ee-Aw's back. Look—he's sorry he galloped away. He won't do it again."

"Where's that Bumpy-Dog?" said Noddy, still looking fierce. "What on earth did he think he was doing? Behaving like that, and upsetting everyone!"

Bumpy was hiding behind the donkey. When he heard Noddy's angry voice he crept out and went to him. He sat up on his hind legs and begged, looking at Noddy out of big, sad eyes.

"He's begging you to forgive him," said Tessie.

"All right," said Noddy. "I forgive you, Bumpy." Bumpy was so overjoyed that he leapt up at Noddy, licking him everywhere—and down went poor Noddy. BUMP!

"Get OFF me, Bumpy!" he groaned. "What a dog! Stop licking me. Tessie, pull him off. I really *must* get on with my work."

7. HURRAY! HURRAY!

NODDY and Ee-Aw worked very hard for three whole days after that. Noddy piled everything on to Ee-Aw's back, and either rode on top or walked beside him. Ee-Aw slept in Noddy's garage every night, and was really very good except that he sometimes took it into his head to gallop at top speed, and poor Noddy had to run till he was quite out of breath.

"Still, you are very useful, Ee-Aw," said Noddy. "I think I've enough money now to pay for my car being mended. Oh, I WISH my little car was back. I do miss it so. I went to look at it yesterday, Ee-Aw, and it looked dreadful — its wheels were off, and its hooter was gone, and —

and — no, I mustn't think about it, or I'll start to howl like Bumpy does when *he's* upset."

56

HURRAY! HURRAY!

The next day Noddy had a shock! The Saucepan Man arrived very suddenly, clanking and clinking as usual. "Where's Ee-Aw?" he said. "I want him. I've missed him so much. I've come to take him back."

"But Mr Saucepan! I thought I would have him till my little car was mended!" said Noddy. "Didn't you go to see your Aunt Katie Kettle?"

"No. I was seasick on the boat, and turned back," said Mr Saucepan. "Where's Ee-Aw?"

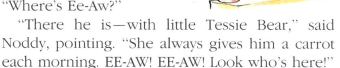

"There he is—with little Tessie Bear," said Noddy, pointing. "She always gives him a carrot each morning. EE-AW! EE-AW! Look who's here!"

Well, Ee-Aw was delighted to see the old Saucepan Man again. He galloped up at top speed and almost knocked him over, ee-awing so loudly that everyone looked out of their windows to see what the noise could be. Mr Saucepan put his arms round Ee-Aw's neck, and they went off up the street, without even saying goodbye to little

CHEER UP LITTLE NODDY!

Noddy! They were so pleased to be together again!

Noddy felt left out and lonely. *Now* what was he to do? He couldn't pull that heavy handcart again, or wheel that big barrow. He sat down on the kerb, feeling sad. "Ee-Aw *might* have said goodbye to me," he thought. "Oh dear—how miserable I feel without my dear little car!"

But look, Noddy—look what's coming down the street, all by itself, looking for you! It's been to your little House-For-One, and you weren't there. It looked into the garage but that was empty. It went up to Big-Ears' house, and there was no

one there either. Noddy lift your head, and see what's coming down the street!

But Noddy didn't lift his head. He sat on the kerb, looking very sad. Then he felt something nudge him, and he heard a soft little sound in his ear. "Parp-parp!"

Ah—*then* he looked up! A big smile came over his face, and he leapt to his feet. "My little car! You're mended! You've come to find me!

HURRAY! HURRAY!

You look BEAUTIFUL! Oh, I'm *so* happy!"

"Parp-parp," said the little car, and jiggled about all round Noddy. Then it butted him gently, and opened one of its doors all by itself.

"Yes, yes—I'm going to get in and drive you!" said Noddy, joyfully. "Just let me look at you for a minute—you look so fine, so clean, so shiny! Oh, I've missed you so! Have you missed *me*, little car?"

"PARP-PARP-PARP!" said the car very loudly indeed, and jiggled about again. Noddy jumped into the driving seat, and drove away down the street, singing loudly. The little car hooted, and everyone came running to their doors and windows to see what was happening.

"It's Noddy! He's got his car back! It's mended. Hurray! Hurray!"

CHEER UP LITTLE NODDY!

Noddy drove all round Toy Town singing at the top of his voice. It was such a happy song. Listen!

"My car is mended, it's good as new,
Parp-parp!
If you want a ride, it's ready for you,
Parp-parp!
We'll take you wherever you want to go,
We'll drive you fast and we'll drive you slow,
PARP-PARP-PARP!
So hurry along and jump inside,
Hurray!
You'll have a perfectly lovely ride,
Hurray!
Oh, we're so happy, my car and I,
We can't HELP singing as we go by,
HURRAY! HURRAY!"

THE NODDY LIBRARY

1. NODDY GOES TO TOYLAND
2. HURRAH FOR LITTLE NODDY
3. NODDY AND HIS CAR
4. HERE COMES NODDY AGAIN!
5. WELL DONE NODDY!
6. NODDY GOES TO SCHOOL
7. NODDY AT THE SEASIDE
8. NODDY GETS INTO TROUBLE
9. NODDY AND THE MAGIC RUBBER
10. YOU FUNNY LITTLE NODDY
11. NODDY MEETS FATHER CHRISTMAS
12. NODDY AND TESSIE BEAR
13. BE BRAVE LITTLE NODDY!
14. NODDY AND THE BUMPY-DOG
15. DO LOOK OUT NODDY!
16. YOU'RE A GOOD FRIEND NODDY!
17. NODDY HAS AN ADVENTURE
18. NODDY GOES TO SEA
19. NODDY AND THE BUNKEY
20. CHEER UP LITTLE NODDY!
21. NODDY GOES TO THE FAIR
22. MR PLOD AND LITTLE NODDY
23. NODDY AND THE TOOTLES
24. NODDY AND THE AEROPLANE